# THE ALIEN INVASION

**Karen Lewis**
**The Alien Invasion**

All rights reserved
Copyright © 2024 by Karen Lewis

No part of this publication may be reproduced, distributed, or
transmitted in any form or by any means, including photocopying,
recording, or other electronic or mechanical methods, without the
prior written permission of the publisher, except in the case of brief
quotations embodied in critical reviews and certain other
noncommercial uses permitted by copyright law.

Published by Spines
ISBN: 979-8-89383-483-3

# THE ALIEN INVASION

KAREN LEWIS

CHAPTER

# ONE

## Aliens

In the small town of Greenfield, a series of strange occurrences began to unsettle the residents. Reports of mysterious lights in the sky, unexplained disappearances, and eerie sightings of strange figures lurking in the shadows spread like wildfire. The townspeople whispered of alien abductions and government cover-ups, their fear growing with each passing day.

A group of friends, including Sarah, Jake, and Alex, decided to investigate the strange happenings in Greenfield. Armed with cameras, flashlights, and a sense of curiosity, they ventured into the dark woods on the outskirts of town, where most of the sightings had been reported.

## The Woods

As they delved deeper into the woods, a sense of unease settled over the group. Strange noises echoed through the trees, and an otherworldly chill hung in the air. Suddenly, a blinding light illuminated the clearing ahead, and the friends found themselves face-to-face with a massive, metallic spaceship hovering above them.

Panic set in as the friends realized they were not alone. Alien beings, with twisted, grotesque forms and glowing eyes, emerged from the shadows, surrounding the group. Sarah, Jake, and Alex tried to run, but they were quickly captured by the aliens and dragged aboard the spaceship.

## The Alien Vessel

Inside the alien vessel, the friends were subjected to horrifying experiments and tests, their screams echoing through the cold, metallic corridors. They witnessed other captives, their bodies twisted and mutilated by the cruel hands of their extraterrestrial captors.

Sarah, Jake, and Alex knew they had to escape before they suffered the same fate. They banded together, using their wits and resourcefulness to outsmart the alien guards and find a way off the ship. As they navigated the labyrinthine corridors, they uncovered the dark truth behind the aliens' sinister agenda - to harvest human bodies for experimentation and genetic manipulation.

## Escape

With time running out and the aliens closing in, the friends made a daring escape, fighting their way through the ship's defenses and reaching the exit just as the spaceship began to lift off. As they tumbled out into the night sky, they watched in horror as the spaceship disappeared into the darkness, leaving behind a trail of destruction and despair.

Sarah, Jake, and Alex returned to Greenfield, forever changed by their harrowing encounter with the extraterrestrial beings. They knew that the truth about aliens was far more terrifying than they could have ever imagined, and that the horrors they had witnessed would haunt them for the rest of their days. The town of Greenfield would never be the same, its once peaceful streets forever tainted by the lingering presence of the alien threat that lurked just beyond the stars.

**Alien ships**

The night was dark and foreboding, the moon hidden behind thick clouds as a strange, eerie glow illuminated the sky. People around the world looked up in horror as massive alien ships descended from the heavens, unleashing a barrage of destructive energy beams that decimated entire cities in moments.

Panic spread like wildfire as the aliens, grotesque and otherworldly in appearance, began their merciless onslaught on Earth. The ground shook with each devastating blast, buildings crumbled, and screams of terror filled the air.

Governments tried to mount a defense, but it was futile against the overwhelming power of the alien invaders. People ran for their lives, desperate to escape the destruction raining down from above.

CHAPTER

# TWO

## Survivors

In the chaos, a group of survivors banded together, determined to fight back against the alien menace. Armed with whatever weapons they could scavenge, they launched a daring guerrilla campaign against the invaders, striking from the shadows and using their wits to outsmart the technologically superior aliens.

But as the days turned into weeks, hope began to fade. The aliens seemed unstoppable, their relentless assault leaving the Earth a smoldering wasteland of death and despair.

**Mission**

In a final, desperate gambit, the survivors launched a daring mission to infiltrate the alien mothership and destroy it from within. It was a suicide mission, but they knew it was their only hope for survival.

As they fought their way through the twisted corridors of the alien ship, they faced unimaginable horrors and overwhelming odds. But in a moment of sacrifice and bravery, they managed to trigger a chain reaction that tore the mothership apart in a blinding explosion of light.

## Survivors

The survivors watched in awe as the alien ships retreated, their once-mighty armada now shattered and broken. Earth was scarred and wounded, but the invaders had been defeated.

As the dust settled and the survivors emerged from the rubble, they knew that they had paid a heavy price for their victory. But they also knew that they had proven that humanity would not go down without a fight, no matter how terrifying the enemy.

# THREE

## Destroying Earth

And as they looked to the stars, they vowed to rebuild and reclaim their world, never forgetting the harrowing night when aliens had tried to destroy Earth, but had ultimately failed.

Sarah, Jake, and Alex had joined forces with a group of survivors in a desperate attempt to stop the aliens from completely destroying the Earth. The team came up with a plan to take down the alien mothership, hoping that it would put an end to the invasion once and for all.

## The Mothership

As they made their way to the mothership, the group encountered unimaginable horrors. The aliens seemed to be everywhere, their tentacles reaching out to grab anyone in their path. Buildings crumbled around them as the aliens wreaked havoc on the city, leaving destruction and death in their wake.

Sarah, Jake, and Alex fought bravely alongside their new allies, using all their skills and resources to push forward towards the mothership. But just as they were getting closer to their goal, disaster struck.

**Explosion**

A massive explosion rocked the ground beneath their feet, causing the team to be separated and trapped in different parts of the city. Sarah found herself surrounded by a horde of aliens, their slimy tentacles closing in on her. Jake and Alex were nowhere to be seen, and she feared the worst.

Frantically searching for a way out, Sarah stumbled upon a hidden underground tunnel that seemed to lead toward the mothership. With no other options left, she plunged into the darkness, hoping against hope that she would find a way to reunite with her friends and stop the aliens before it was too late.

## Aliens

As she made her way through the winding tunnels, Sarah could hear the eerie screeches of the aliens echoing around her. She knew that time was running out, and the fate of the Earth rested on her shoulders. With determination in her heart, Sarah prepared to face whatever horrors lay ahead and do whatever it took to save her friends and the world from the impending doom of the alien invasion.

# FOUR

Sarah, Jake, and Alex continued their treacherous journey through the underground tunnels, determined to find their friends and put an end to the alien invasion. The dimly lit passageways were filled with eerie whispers and strange, otherworldly sounds that sent shivers down their spines.

As they navigated through the labyrinthine tunnels, they encountered other survivors who had been trapped by the aliens. Sarah, Jake, and Alex vowed to help them, banding together to fight off the alien creatures that lurked in the shadows.

## Passing moment

With each passing moment, the group grew closer to their friends who had been taken captive by the aliens. The stakes were high, but they knew they had to push forward, no matter the danger that lay ahead.

Finally, after what felt like an eternity, they reached the heart of the mothership. It was a massive, twisted structure that pulsated with an otherworldly energy. The aliens swarmed around them, their grotesque forms moving in a synchronized dance of death and destruction.

**Aliens**

Sarah, Jake, and Alex fought valiantly, using all their skills and cunning to outsmart the aliens and free their captured friends. With each alien they defeated, they inched closer to their goal, driven by the hope of saving not only their friends but also the entire planet from annihilation.

As the final showdown with the alien queen loomed ahead, Sarah, Jake, and Alex knew that their united strength and determination were their best weapons. Together, they would face the ultimate horror of the alien invasion and emerge victorious, saving their friends and the Earth from the clutches of the extraterrestrial menace.

# FIVE

## Labyrinths

Labyrinths, with traps and dangers at every turn. The group of survivors must navigate carefully, using whatever means necessary to stay alive.

As they travel deeper into the tunnels, they encounter strange creatures that lurk in the shadows, ready to pounce at any moment. The group must stick together and watch each other's backs, for the slightest misstep could mean certain death.

The air grows thick and musty, making it difficult to breathe. The darkness is suffocating, and the constant fear of the unknown weighs heavily on their minds.

Despite the odds stacked against them, the group pushes forward, driven by the hope of finding a way out of this hellish maze. They know that they must stay strong and united if they have any chance of surviving this treacherous journey through the underground tunnels.

## Survivors

As Sarah, Jake, Alex, and the group of survivors cautiously approach the end of the hellish tunnel, they can sense the presence of the aliens waiting for them. The survivors exchange nervous glances, knowing that they are about to face a formidable and unknown enemy.

As they emerge into a large cavern at the end of the tunnel, the aliens come into view, their eerie forms illuminated by an otherworldly glow. The survivors stand their ground, weapons at the ready, preparing to defend themselves against this alien threat.

## CHAPTER
# SIX

### The chance

The aliens move closer, their movements fluid and menacing. Sarah, Jake, Alex, and the survivors know that they must work together to stand a chance against this formidable foe. With adrenaline pumping and hearts racing, they prepare to engage in a battle for their lives.

As the aliens launch their attack, a fierce and chaotic battle ensues. The survivors fight with all their strength, using every ounce of skill and courage they possess to fend off the alien invaders. The cavern echoes with the sounds of gunfire, alien screeches, and the shouts of the survivors as they struggle to overcome this otherworldly menace.

## Determination

Through sheer determination and teamwork, Sarah, Jake, Alex, and the survivors manage to hold their own against the aliens. Slowly but surely, they gain the upper hand, driving the aliens back and forcing them to retreat.

As the last of the aliens slink away into the shadows, the survivors catch their breath, relieved but wary. They know that this battle is far from over, and that they must remain vigilant as they continue their journey through the dark and treacherous tunnels. But for now, they can take a moment to regroup and celebrate their hard-won victory against the alien threat.

# SEVEN

As the survivors continued their journey through the tunnels, they remained on high alert, knowing that the alien threat could resurface at any moment. Despite their vigilance, a month later, their worst fears were realized as the aliens returned with a vengeance.

The survivors were caught off guard by the sudden reappearance of the aliens, who launched a coordinated and relentless attack. Sarah, Jake, Alex, and the group of survivors found themselves once again facing the formidable foe that had haunted their nightmares since the beginning of their harrowing journey.

Determined not to be defeated, the survivors fought back with all their might, their weapons blazing as they tried to fend off the alien invaders. The cavern echoed with the sounds of battle, a cacophony of gunfire, alien screeches, and the shouts of the survivors as they struggled to hold their ground.

Despite their best efforts, the survivors soon found themselves overwhelmed by the sheer numbers and ferocity of the alien attackers. Sarah, Jake, Alex, and the others fought bravely, but it soon became clear that they were outnumbered and outmatched.

As the aliens closed in, the survivors knew that they were facing almost certain defeat. But just as all hope seemed lost, a sudden explosion rocked the cavern, causing chaos among the alien ranks.

## Chaos

In the midst of the chaos, a group of mysterious figures emerged, armed to the teeth and ready to join the fight. With their help, the survivors were able to turn the tide of battle, pushing back the alien invaders and driving them into retreat once more.

# EIGHT

## The Mothership

Exhausted but victorious, Sarah, Jake, Alex, and the survivors regrouped, grateful for the timely intervention that had saved them from certain doom. As they caught their breath and tended to their wounds, they knew that the battle was far from over, but they also knew that they had the strength and determination to face whatever challenges lay ahead.

As the survivors regrouped and caught their breath after the intense battle, they couldn't help but wonder about the mysterious figures who had come to their aid. These newcomers possessed advanced technology that seemed to be beyond anything the survivors had ever seen before.

## Newcomers

The newcomers introduced themselves as the "Guardians," a group of warriors who had been tracking the alien threat for years. They explained that they had been monitoring the survivors' progress and had intervened when they saw that the aliens had launched another attack.

**Guardians**

The Guardians' technology was truly mesmerizing to the survivors. They wielded energy weapons that could cut through the alien creatures with ease, and their armor seemed to be impervious to the aliens' attacks. The survivors watched in awe as the Guardians effortlessly dispatched the alien threat, their movements precise and coordinated.

# NINE

## Aliens

As the survivors spoke with the Guardians, they learned that the aliens were not just mindless creatures, but part of a larger, more sinister force that threatened not only Earth but the entire galaxy. The Guardians had been fighting this threat for centuries, and they knew that the survivors would need their help if they were to stand a chance against the alien menace.

**Guardians**

With the Guardians by their side, the survivors felt a newfound sense of hope and determination. They knew that they were not alone in this fight and that they had powerful allies who were willing to stand with them against the alien threat.

Armed with their newfound knowledge and the advanced technology of the Guardians, Sarah, Jake, Alex, and the survivors prepared for the battles that lay ahead. They knew that the road would be long and treacherous, but with the Guardians at their side, they were ready to face whatever challenges came their way.

## Aliens

The Guardians activated their advanced tracking technology, which allowed them to pinpoint the location of the alien creatures with precision. Using their sophisticated sensors and scanners, they were able to detect the aliens' movements and anticipate their next moves.

The Guardians shared this information with the survivors, who quickly formulated a plan to launch a preemptive strike against the aliens. With the Guardians leading the way, the survivors moved swiftly and stealthily toward the aliens' lair, using the tracking technology to avoid detection.

**Attack**

As they approached the aliens' stronghold, the survivors and the Guardians prepared for a fierce battle. The Guardians' energy weapons crackled with power, ready to unleash devastating blasts against the alien creatures. The survivors braced themselves for the coming fight, knowing that their newfound allies would be crucial in turning the tide of the battle.

With the element of surprise on their side, the survivors and the Guardians launched their attack, catching the aliens off guard. The Guardians' advanced technology proved to be a game-changer, as they swiftly neutralized the alien threat with their superior firepower and tactics.

## Survivors

The survivors fought alongside the Guardians, their courage and determination bolstered by the knowledge that they had powerful allies fighting by their side. Together, they pushed back the alien forces, driving them back and securing a hard-fought victory.

## Guardians

As the dust settled and the survivors caught their breath, they knew that they owed their success to the Guardians and their advanced technology. With their tracking capabilities and combat prowess, the Guardians had proven to be invaluable allies in the fight against the alien menace. And as they prepared to face future challenges, the survivors were grateful to have the Guardians watching their back.

## Vampires

The Guardians were shocked to discover that the aliens had brought extraterrestrial vampires from a distant planet to Earth with the intention of colonizing it. These extraterrestrial vampires were unlike anything the Guardians had ever encountered before – they possessed advanced technology and supernatural abilities that made them a formidable threat.

The extraterrestrial vampires were able to move swiftly and silently, blending into the shadows and striking their prey with deadly precision. They had the ability to drain the life force of their victims, leaving them weak and vulnerable. The Guardians knew that they had to act quickly to prevent the extraterrestrial vampires from taking over Earth and enslaving humanity.

**Despite**

Despite the challenges they faced, the Guardians were determined to protect Earth and its inhabitants from this new threat. They mobilized their forces and used their advanced technology to track down the extraterrestrial vampires and engage them in battle. It was a fierce and intense struggle, but the Guardians were able to defeat the extraterrestrial vampires and drive them back to their distant planet.

After the battle was won, the Guardians vowed to remain vigilant and continue to protect Earth from any future threats that may arise. They knew that the universe was vast and full of dangers, but they were committed to ensuring the safety and well-being of all living beings on Earth.

**Success**

However, just when the Guardians thought they had successfully defeated the extraterrestrial vampires, a new horror emerged. The extraterrestrial vampires had unleashed a powerful ancient entity known as the Shadow Queen, a being of pure darkness and malevolence.

The Shadow Queen was a formidable foe, capable of manipulating shadows and darkness to her advantage. She had the ability to corrupt and control the minds of others, turning them into mindless minions to do her bidding. The Guardians realized that they were facing a threat unlike anything they had ever encountered before.

# ELEVEN

## Vampires

As the Shadow Queen's influence spread, the Guardians knew that they had to act quickly to stop her before she could plunge the world Into eternal darkness. They gathered their strength and courage, ready to face the Shadow Queen in a final battle for the fate of Earth.

The battle against the Shadow Queen was fierce and intense, with the Guardians using all of their powers and abilities to combat her dark forces. The fate of Earth hung in the balance as the Guardians fought with all their might to defeat the Shadow Queen and save humanity from her evil grasp.

**Victorious**

In the end, the Guardians emerged victorious, banishing the Shadow Queen back to the depths of the universe from whence she came. They knew that they had faced a great evil and had prevailed, but they also understood that the universe was vast and full of unknown dangers.

The Guardians vowed to remain vigilant, ready to face whatever challenges may come their way and protect Earth from any threat that dared to endanger it. They stood united, a beacon of hope and light in a universe filled with darkness and uncertainty.

**Earth**

As the Guardians continued to monitor the situation on Earth, they soon discovered that the extraterrestrial vampires had not been completely defeated. In fact, they had managed to infiltrate human society and were now using their mind-controlling abilities to slowly colonize and manipulate unsuspecting individuals.

## Guardians

The Guardians knew that they had to act quickly to prevent the extraterrestrial vampires from gaining a foothold on Earth and enslaving its population.

They mobilized their forces and began a covert operation to root out the vampires' influence and protect humanity from their insidious plans.

The Guardians used their unique powers and skills to identify and neutralize the vampires' human hosts, freeing them from the creatures' control and preventing further colonization. They worked tirelessly to uncover the vampires' hidden strongholds and eliminate them one by one, ensuring that Earth remained safe from their dark influence.

## Extraterrestrial Vampires

Despite the extraterrestrial vampires' best efforts to expand their control, the Guardians' determination and bravery proved to be too much for them to overcome. With each victory, the Guardians pushed back against the vampires' colonization efforts, ultimately driving them back into hiding and securing Earth's future.

# TWELVE

## Guardians

The Guardians knew that the threat of the extraterrestrial vampires would always loom over Earth, but they remained vigilant and prepared to defend humanity against any future incursions. They stood as protectors of the planet, ready to face any challenge that came their way and ensure that Earth remained a beacon of light in the vast darkness of the universe.

## Aliens

The alien visitors were initially intrigued by the extraterrestrial vampires, fascinated by their unique physiology and abilities. However, as they spent more time with the vampires, they began to realize the true extent of their danger.

The vampires were not like the creatures of myth and legend on Earth. They were ruthless predators, feeding on the life force of any living being they encountered. Their powers of mind control and shape-shifting made them even more formidable opponents.

**Humans**

The humans, who had initially welcomed the alien visitors with open arms, now found themselves in a desperate battle for survival. The vampires had already begun to infiltrate human society, using their powers to manipulate and control key figures in government and law enforcement.

As the situation escalated, the alien visitors and humans were forced to band together to fight off the vampire threat. It was a battle unlike anything they had ever faced before, with the fate of both species hanging in the balance.

## Conflict

In the end, it was a close and bloody conflict, but with the combined strength and ingenuity of the alien visitors and humans, they were able to defeat the extraterrestrial vampires and drive them from Earth.

The battle against the extraterrestrial vampires was indeed a brutal and bloody affair. The vampires, with their superior strength and powers, proved to be formidable opponents. Many lives were lost on both sides as the conflict raged on.

**Aliens**

The aliens and humans fought with all their might, utilizing advanced technology and tactics to try to gain the upper hand. The vampires, however, were cunning and ruthless, using their mind-control abilities to sow chaos and confusion among their enemies.

As the battle reached its climax, the streets ran red with blood as the casualties mounted. The once peaceful cityscape was transformed into a war zone, with buildings reduced to rubble and the sounds of battle echoing through the night.

## The Forces

Despite the overwhelming odds, the combined forces of the aliens and humans refused to back down. They fought with courage and determination, knowing that the fate of Earth and all its inhabitants hung in the balance.

Finally, after a long and grueling struggle, the tide began to turn. The aliens and humans managed to exploit a weakness in the vampires' defenses, turning the tide of the battle in their favor. With a final, coordinated assault, they were able to drive the extraterrestrial vampires back and secure victory.

# THIRTEEN

Page 47.

Aftermath

The aftermath of the battle was somber, with many lives lost and the city in ruins. But the aliens and humans stood united, proud of their hard-won victory and grateful to have survived the ordeal. The experience had forged a bond between the two species, a shared history of sacrifice and triumph that would never be forgotten.

As the extraterrestrial vampires launched their relentless assault on the city, the humans found themselves overwhelmed and outnumbered. Despite their best efforts and valiant resistance, the sheer numbers and superior abilities of the vampires proved too much to handle.

**Aliens**

The humans fought bravely, but the vampires' mind-control powers and deadly strength proved to be too formidable. The streets were quickly overrun, with chaos and destruction reigning supreme as the vampires hunted down their prey with ruthless efficiency.

The city fell Into despair as the humans struggled to defend themselves against the overwhelming force of the vampires. Many lives were lost, and the survivors were forced to retreat and seek refuge wherever they could find it.

## Vampires

As the vampires tightened their grip on the city, the humans realized that they were facing an enemy unlike anything they had ever encountered before. With their backs against the wall and their resources dwindling, the humans knew that they were fighting a losing battle.

In the end, the extraterrestrial vampires emerged victorious, their reign of terror unchallenged as they established their dominance over the city. The humans, devastated and defeated, were forced to accept their new reality as subjects of the vampire overlords.

**The City**

The once vibrant and bustling city now lay in ruins, a grim reminder of the price of defeat in the face of an unstoppable enemy. The humans vowed to never forget the sacrifice of those who had fallen in the battle against the vampires, and they held onto the hope that one day, they would rise again to reclaim their home from the clutches of their extraterrestrial oppressors.

vampires had proven to be a formidable and terrifying force, one that the humans had never encountered before. Their advanced technology, supernatural abilities, and sheer numbers had overwhelmed the human defenders, leaving them devastated and defeated.

The humans knew that they needed to regroup and come up with a new strategy if they were to have any hope of defeating the extraterrestrial vampires. They sought out any remaining survivors, rallying them together to form a resistance movement against their otherworldly foes.

# FOURTEEN

As they planned their next move, the humans scoured the city for any resources they could use to their advantage. They scavenged for weapons, technology, and supplies, knowing that they would need every possible advantage in their fight against the extraterrestrial vampires.

The resistance fighters trained tirelessly, honing their skills and preparing themselves for the inevitable confrontation with the vampires. They knew that the odds were stacked against them, but they refused to give up hope and were determined to reclaim their city from the extraterrestrial invaders.

# FIFTEEN

When the time came, the humans launched a daring counterattack against the extraterrestrial vampires. They used guerrilla tactics, ambushes, and traps to catch the vampires off guard and exploit their weaknesses.

Despite the vampires' superior abilities, the humans fought with fierce determination and unwavering resolve. They refused to back down, knowing that their freedom and survival depended on their ability to defeat the extraterrestrial vampires.

In a climactic battle, the humans finally emerged victorious, driving the extraterrestrial vampires out of the city and reclaiming their homes. The vampires, weakened and demoralized, retreated back to their own world, defeated by the resilience and courage of the human resistance.

The city, once again free from the grip of the extraterrestrial vampires, began to rebuild and recover from the devastation of the battle. The humans, united in their victory, celebrated their hard-won triumph, and vowed to never again let their city fall under the control of such a terrifying enemy.

# SIXTEEN

As the humans were celebrating their victory over the extraterrestrial vampires, a new threat emerged from the skies. Alien spacecraft descended upon the city, their advanced technology far surpassing anything the humans had ever seen.

At first, the humans feared that the aliens had come to conquer and destroy them as well. But to their surprise, the aliens began attacking the extraterrestrial vampires, engaging them in a fierce battle that shook the city to its core.

The aliens' weapons were powerful and their tactics were strategic, catching the vampires off guard and turning the tide of the battle in favor of the humans. It soon became clear that the aliens had their own reasons for intervening in the conflict, and they were determined to rid the city of the extraterrestrial vampires once and for all.

The humans watched in awe as the aliens and the vampires clashed in a spectacular display of technology and supernatural abilities. The battle raged on for hours, with explosions lighting up the sky and the ground trembling beneath their feet.

CHAPTER

# SEVENTEEN

In the end, the aliens emerged victorious, driving the remaining extraterrestrial vampires back to their world and sealing the portal through which they had come. With the threat of the vampires finally eliminated, the aliens turned to the humans and offered their assistance in rebuilding the city and ensuring its protection from any future threats.

Grateful for the aliens' help, the humans welcomed them as allies and worked together to restore the city to its former glory. The humans and the aliens forged a new alliance, united in their determination to defend their home against any who would seek to harm it.